Do You See Mouse?

Do You See Mouse?

Story by Marion Crume
Pictures by Normand L. Chartier

Silver Press
Parsippany, New Jersey

© 1995 Silver Burdett Press
Illustrations © 1995 Normand L. Chartier

© Copyright, 1985, 1974, by Ginn and Company
Theodore Clymer, adviser

Published by Silver Press, an imprint of Silver Burdett Press,
A Simon and Schuster Company
299 Jefferson Road, Parsippany, NJ 07054

Printed in the United States of America
10 9 8 7 6 5 4 3 2 1

Library of Congress Cataloging-in-Publication Data
Crume, Marion W.
Do You See Mouse? / by Marion Crume;
illustrated by Normand L. Chartier.   p. cm.
Summary: When the animals play hide-and-seek,
Turtle finds all of them easily except for Mouse.
ISBN 0-382-24683-7 (LSB) ISBN 0-382-24684-5 (JHC)
ISBN 0-382-24685-3 (S/C)
[1. Hide-and-seek--Fiction. 2. Animals--Fiction.]
I. Chartier, Normand, 1945-   ill. II. Title.
PZ7.C8883Do 1995
[E]--dc20   94-30494   CIP   AC

"**W**ho wants to play hide and seek?" said Mouse.

"I do," said Elephant.

"I do," said Parrot.

"I do," said Lion.

"And I will be IT," said Turtle.

"We will look for places to hide," said Elephant.

"And I will look for you," said Turtle.

"...1...2..."

"I can hide here," said Elephant.
And he did.

"I can hide here," said Parrot.
And he did.

"...3...4..."

"I can hide here," said Lion.
And he did.

Mouse said, "I do not see a place to hide."

"...5...6..."

"Elephant, let me hide with you," said Mouse.
"No, you can't hide here," said Elephant.

"Parrot, let me hide with you," said Mouse.
"No, you can't hide here," said Parrot.

"…7…8…"

"Lion, let me hide with you," said Mouse.

"No, you can't hide here," said Lion.

". . . 9 . . . 10 . . .
Here I come."

"I see you, Elephant," said Turtle.
"You can't hide from me."

"I see you, Parrot," said Turtle.
"You can't hide from me."

"I see you, too, Lion," said Turtle.

"You can't hide from me."

"But I do not see Mouse," said Turtle.

"Do you see Mouse?"

"Yes," said the animals. "We see Mouse."

"You do?" said Turtle.

"Here I am," shouted Mouse!